Ladybird I'm **Ready...**
for Phonics!

Note to parents, carers and teachers

Ladybird I'm Ready for Phonics is a series of phonic reading books that have been carefully written to give gradual, structured practice of the synthetic phonics programme your child is learning at school.

Each book focuses on a set of phonemes (sounds) together with their graphemes (letters). The books also provide practice of common tricky words, such as **the** and **said**, that cannot be sounded out.

The series closely follows the order that your child is taught phonics in school, from initial letter sounds to key phonemes and beyond. It helps to build reading confidence through practice of these phonics building blocks, and reinforces school learning in a fun way.

Ideas for use

- Children learn best when reading is a fun experience. Read the book together and give your child plenty of praise and encouragement.

- Help your child identify and sound out the phonemes (sounds) in any words he is having difficulty reading. Then, blend these sounds together to read the word.

- Talk about the story words and tricky words at the end of each story to reinforce learning.

For more information and advice on synthetic phonics and school book banding, visit **www.ladybird.com/phonics**

Book Band 2

Level 7 builds on the sounds learnt in levels 1 to 6 and introduces new sounds and their letter representations:

ai   ee   oa   oo   oo
                    (long)   (short)

Special features:

repetition of sounds in different words

short sentences with simple language

summary page to reinforce learning

Written by Catherine Baker
Illustrated by Chris Jevons

Phonics and Book Banding Consultant: Kate Ruttle

A catalogue record for this book is available from the British Library

Published by Ladybird Books Ltd
80 Strand, London, WC2R 0RL
A Penguin Company

001

ISBN: 978-0-72327-543-5
Printed in China

Ladybird I'm Ready...
for Phonics!

The Big Fish

Jack and Jen sail off
in a boat.

7

9

Jack and Jen zoom off
to see the fish.

Can you see
that big eel, Jack?

11

Jen looks for big fish.

But then a big, big fish sees her, too.

Jen, quick! We need to go!

The big fish zooms up to
Jack and Jen. But it did
not get them.

Get back on
the boat, Jack!

Story Words

Can you match these words
to the pictures below?

boat	Jen
fish	sail
Jack	eel

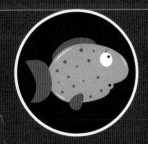

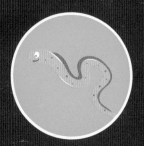

Tricky Words

These tricky words are in the story you have just read. They cannot be phonetically sounded out. Can you memorize them and read them super fast?

we	you
go	the
they	was
to	
her	
me	

Ladybird I'm Ready... for Phonics!

The Big Ship

Jen and Jack sail off on the boat.

I can not wait!

21

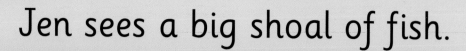

Jen sees a big shoal of fish.

I need to get a good shot of the fish.

23

They see no fish in the ship, but they can see a big box!

The box has loads of rings and things in it.

29

Story Words

Can you match these words to the pictures below?

fish   box

shoal   ring

ship

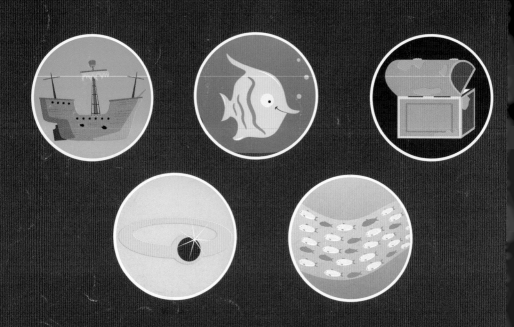

Tricky Words

These tricky words are in the story you have just read. They cannot be phonetically sounded out. Can you memorize them and read them super fast?

the	be
we	they
I	me
my	no
to	

Collect all
Ladybird I'm Ready...
for Phonics!

Captain Comet's
Space Party
9780723275374

9780723275381

Top Dog
9780723275398

Huff! Puff! Run!
9780723275404

Fix It Vets
9780723275411

Dash is Fab!
9780723275428

Big, Big Fish
9780723275435

Dig, Farmer, Dig!
9780723275442

Fun Fair Fun
9780723275459

Wow, Wowzer!
9780723275466

Wizard Woody
9780723275473

Monster Stars
9780723275480

Say the Sounds
9780723271598

Flashcards
9780723272069

Available on the **App Store**

Ladybird I'm Ready for...
apps are now available for
iPad, iPhone and iPod touch.

Apps also available on Android devices